MANTRAP

Danny wanted to whoop and holler. *More meat. More delicious juices running down his throat.* Then the darkness flashed white and he was blinded.

'Got you!' said the voice inside the light. Danny heard the metallic click of a safety catch released. 'Dadda!'

Look out for other exciting stories
in the *Shades* series:

SHADES

MANTRAP

Tish Farrell

Evans

Published by Evans Brothers Limited
2A Portman Mansions
Chiltern St
London W1U 6NR

First published in 2007

British Library Cataloguing in Publication Data
Farrel, Tish
Mantrap. - (Shades)
1. Young adult fiction
I. Title
823. 9'2 [J]

ISBN 0 237 53203 4
13-digit ISBN 978 0 237 53203 1

Series Editor: David Orme
Editor: Julia Moffatt
Designer: Rob Walster

Contents

Chapter One
The Kill

Impala! A small herd among the sausage trees. Jacob stopped dead and held up a warning hand. Danny froze on the spot and this time, without a sound, dropped behind a potato bush. He peered through the leaves, fixing on the big ram. He was about twenty paces away, grazing the yellow grasses, his harem of females all round. Danny's eyes stung with longing. There was that beautiful ram! So near, and yet so far. The smallest sound might send him bolting. Out of reach!

Danny willed Jacob to shoot. *Now, Dadda, now.* Then nearly howled when the ram raised his lyre-shaped horns and sniffed the breeze nervously. The ram scented them. He had. Danny prayed and prayed. *Please let our luck change. Please let Dadda shoot. Then we can get out of here. Before the sun comes up. Before the park rangers start their patrol. Before we're caught and sent to jail...*

He held his breath till it burned in his chest and prayed some more: *And please don't let me foul up this time. Please, please, please...*

It was all right. The ram put his head down and went on grazing. The females followed suit. Danny clenched his teeth to stop them chattering. The teeth that had eaten no meat for months, or little else for that matter. Only wild mangoes and the wizened corncobs that the baboons hadn't stolen from their brick-hard fields. The drought went on and on. Relentless. Day after day, month on month, the sun's yellow eye burned down.

From the corner of his own eye Danny now watched Jacob. He was about ten paces away to Danny's left, standing still as stone behind a winter thorn. In the pre-dawn gloom, Danny couldn't see the look on his father's face. He didn't need to. Every line of Jacob's profile said concentration. Now he was slowly slipping an arrow from the quiver inside his shirt, fitting it to the bow, flexing the gut string. Danny bit his lip, his heart beating louder and louder. He started to panic. Couldn't Dadda hear Danny's heart? Wouldn't it spook the impala, just as he had spoiled their chance of a juicy warthog back at the lagoon?

Shoot, Dadda, shoot.

Danny stopped breathing as he thought of the lost warthog. How could he have been so stupid? The warthog had been like a gift. There it was, near the park boundary where there was usually so little game. He and Dadda were downwind, and the boar down on its knees, and too busy digging and chewing roots to spot them. Danny couldn't take his eyes off the meaty rump, his mouth flooding with saliva. Any minute, he thought, they'd have the boar home and in sweet sizzling chunks over the hearth.

He saw Dadda take careful aim, but before the arrow flew, some madness seized Danny. He found himself stepping towards the beast. Somehow his longing for meat had tricked his mind into thinking that the warthog was already theirs. At the sound of his footfall, the boar was off. Tail up, and snorting as he dived into the underbrush. Gone. Danny heard the sigh sift through Jacob's teeth and felt sick to the pit of his own gnawing guts.

To make things worse, his father had said nothing. Not one word of reprimand. But then these days Dadda rarely said much. Just like the sandy streambed where they dug down to their armpits for a dribble of water, Jacob's words had all but dried up.

Danny blinked cold sweat from his eyes, willing the impala to stay. Willing himself too. This time he wouldn't move. Wouldn't. Wouldn't.

Shoot, Dadda. What are you waiting for?

Time spun out and suddenly, like a bad dream the antelope was walking away from them, moving behind an old baobab tree that had been felled by elephants. Danny could only see its head now. He could also see where giant tusks had ripped out the tree's fibrous core. He breathed in suddenly. Another fear. Worse than losing the meat. Elephants. Were they feeding nearby? Had they just torn up this tree?

Do not move. He told himself. *DO NOT MOVE.* Yet the urge to turn round was unbearable. At this very moment a herd of elephants could be creeping up on them, stepping on those silent skull-crushing feet. And – and they could kill him and Dadda as easy as blinking, just as last month they had killed Alice, a neighbour, when she'd tried to stop an old bull from raiding her grain store. The drought was making the big beasts nasty – none of their favourite fresh grass to eat, water-holes drying up. And there were other reasons for them killing humans. Danny drove these thoughts away.

And still Jacob hadn't fired a shot! It seemed he meant to move in closer. (*And risk everything?*) Danny now saw his father take a pinch of dirt from the leather pouch on his belt, watched the red Luangwa dust blow off like lost hope.

Except it wasn't lost, was it? The dirt blowing behind Dadda like that meant the wind was still on their side. It was blowing their scent away from the herd.

Now, Dadda, now. Kill the ram now. Before the breeze turns and he smells us.

Danny blinked again. When he looked once more, Jacob was on the move. Quiet as a ghost he was closing on the herd. Then the arrow flew. Then the herd fled, barking in fear. Then a flock of white storks burst from a thorn tree and stopped Danny's heart. And then somewhere ahead came the drone of a vehicle. A Land Rover? It could only be rangers – on the main park trail, beyond the sausage trees where dawn's first red rays were already glinting.

'Dadda!' Danny gasped. He was almost beside himself. What had happened? Had Dadda shot the antelope? Was it dead or had it run away? He couldn't see for the baobab trunk, for the long grass, for the rangers coming, for the traitor sun! 'Dadda!' For three long seconds Jacob stood in a daze. Then the spell broke and they both flew forward, throwing themselves flat against the baobab. Now Danny was torn in two. He didn't know what to pray for first – for the ram to have fled unharmed if the rangers stopped; for it to be lying stone dead, if they passed by? Please, please, he murmured. It's life or death now. My life, Dadda's, Mammy's…

Chapter Two
Cover Up

Hiding behind the baobab tree, Danny died
a hundred deaths. Just beyond the sausage
trees the Land Rover suddenly slowed.
Gears grated. The engine missed a stroke.
The rangers must have spotted them. Or
were scanning the bush through their
binoculars. They *must* have spotted them
Danny bit his lip harder, this time tasting

his own blood. Then, quite miraculously, the vehicle gathered speed and drove off.

Danny clung to the dewy grass, felt its cold wetness soak through his shirt. Heard his heart beat hard against the hard earth. How long should he give the rangers before he moved? What if they decided to come back? Then he felt a hand on his arm, and glanced fearfully into Jacob's eyes. The dark eyes gave nothing away. 'Come,' his father mouthed.

Danny scrambled to his feet, stared down the track where the rangers had gone. Even in those few moments, day had dawned more brightly. The red dust kicked up by the truck hung in the sausage trees like a veil. But it was all right. They really had gone, headed off towards the main park gate, the truck engine droning no louder than a bee.

Relief flooded Danny's chest, and his legs turned to water. He stumbled like a baby, falling on the baobab, grazing his arms on its elephant-torn bark.

'It's all right, boy,' Jacob murmured, vaulting over the tree. After a moment Danny clambered after him. Suddenly his heart soared. Dadda must have hit the ram.

Sure enough, there in the grass just beyond the baobab, lay the dead impala, an arrow lodged in its heart. In the rising sun the antelope glowed like a copper statue. It couldn't run from them now. But before Danny could savour the moment, Jacob had slit the ram's throat with the flick of his knife, letting the warm blood flow into a nearby porcupine den. Next the blade whipped through the soft pale underbelly, shovelling guts into the hole, setting aside offal, peeling back the copper hide, slicing flesh for Danny to wrap in grass parcels. By now the antelope's black eyes were already growing dull, the flies dancing round in dizzy swarms. Danny brushed them away. Maybe he felt sorry for the dead impala. Maybe he didn't want to share one shred of it, not even with a fly.

Jacob stopped cutting and Danny shot him an anxious look. Was this all the meat they were taking? It seemed so little after all their effort and worry. His father nodded, and again Danny cursed himself for the missed warthog. If they'd got that an hour ago, it would have still been dark enough, and close enough to home to take the whole carcass without risk of being seen. Now though, with the sun up and rangers about, they could hardly walk through the open bush lugging an impala between them. Instead they would have to follow Jacob's other plan and that was risky. Very risky.

First they would have to stash the carcass where no prowling lion or hyena could reach it. And second, they would have to come back for it at nightfall; back into the park when every predator's nose would be up and sniffing for blood. Danny shuddered. He did not like this plan. He wanted all the meat *now*. To take it home *now* to the secrecy of their hut where he could eat and eat and eat.

Most of all, he wanted this dangerous poaching to be over. He wasn't a brave hunter like his father and grandfathers, or his two older brothers, Clement and Isaac. He was a schoolboy dropout whose teacher, Father McGuire used to make him quake whenever he thumped the big Bible and denounced the wickedness of elephant poaching and similar offences.

Danny looked down at the bloody antelope and his guts wrenched as hunger, conscience and fear clashed. Weren't he and Dadda wicked for taking the impala? The new government in Lusaka seemed to think so. Recently they had sent out more armed scouts and rangers to wage war on the commercial ivory poachers. They had arrested men like Dadda too, fathers who hunted only to keep their families alive when the rains failed and their food stores were empty. In the past, Dadda had taken his brothers to hunt for meat. They knew what to do and wouldn't have made mistakes like Danny, but now they had gone far away to Lusaka, looking for work, and hadn't been heard of since.

And so that left Danny – Danny who hadn't the nerve to come back that night to the park where they should not be. To do things they should not do.

Jacob shook Danny's arm.

'Come on!'

He pointed to a clump of trees that stood back from the main track. Together they dragged the carcass to the foot of a mahogany tree. Jacob nodded. This time Danny knew what his job was. This at least was something he could do well. He shinned several metres up the tree until he found a firm foothold. Just above him was a strong forking branch. He hung on to it while Jacob tied a rope around the dead beast's hocks then tossed him the loose end. Danny threw the rope over the branch and back to Jacob. Between them they hauled the ram up the trunk and Danny wedged it safely in the fork. At last. They could go. Delight surged through every vein and he grinned down at his father. Cunning, eh? To disguise their kill as a leopard's larder. But then old-time hunters like Dadda knew all the tricks.

'The rope!' Jacob warned. Danny quickly untied it and shoved it down the back of his pants, then scrambled down the tree. Next they stuffed the meat parcels inside their shirts and Danny wanted to be off home to cook it – but Jacob wagged a finger. No, he said. First they must cover their tracks and remember the spot. Only a fool lost his meat because he couldn't find his stash in the dark.

Danny nodded grudgingly. As he brushed over his footprints with a thorn tree branch, the grass-wrapped meat dug into his empty belly. It was almost too much to bear. He wanted the meat in his mouth, still raw and red and warm...

Slowly, slowly they reversed into the denser cover of the sage-brush, sweeping their footprints away. Then Danny crept after Jacob. Home wasn't far, just over a half-hour's walk to the park boundary. The problem was that these two miles were the riskiest of the park's many hundred miles. Soon they would run out of cover and have to cross open grassland where anyone might spot them. Worse still, their path home ran by the road to the camp where the rangers and their families stayed. Danny cast anguished looks at his father's back. *Please, please don't let the rangers come. Please let us cross the veldt without being seen.*

Yet to Danny's surprise, when they reached the open country where the grasses rippled in a big yellow sea, Jacob stopped and, bold as brass, got out his knife again. Danny almost sobbed. Not more delay. *Please, Dadda.* Then he remembered. This was Jacob's cover in case the rangers did come by, or spotted them leaving the park. Of course. They were cutting grass to mend their roof thatch. It was the time of year for it, and no one minded the farmers coming to the park's edge for that. Danny minded though. He pulled the garden knife from his belt and slashed the grass savagely. The sweat again stung his eyes: would they never get home?

When Dadda said, 'That'll do, boy. Give me the rope now,' he could have screamed with joy. He reached in the back of his pants. No rope. Must have dropped it while he was cutting. He cast around. Jacob frowned: 'Forget it!' They bound the bundles with grass stems, hiding Jacob's bow and arrows inside, then laid them across their shoulders. Danny walked behind as before, eyes darting left and right. This was like a nightmare where you never ever reached your destination. But then at last, after all the longing and fear, there it was, the line of thorn trees by the dried up stream, the road to the ranger's camp, the path that crossed it, their homestead thatch just a stone's throw beyond. Jacob threw Danny a look, the bare twitch of his brow that said, 'Watch your step. We're not safe yet.' Danny nodded, then took a deep breath and hoping against hope, followed his father into the thorns.

Chapter Three
Meat

This time Danny knew he had died and gone to heaven. The sweet smell of roasting meat told him so.

In fact he and Dadda had been very lucky. They hadn't seen a soul when they came out of the thorn trees – no rangers passing on the road, no neighbours on the path or at the stream, digging through sand for a cup of rusty water. Quickly they had slipped through their compound gateway, knocked quietly on the hut door.

Mammy had opened up at once, ushering them inside, shutting the door quickly and slamming across the wooden bolt. At last they were safe. But in that split second before the hut's gloom hugged round, Danny had read many things in his mother's eyes. Fear. Relief. And then the question she couldn't ask because she'd been so against their going poaching. Did you bring meat, those eyes asked? Yes, Danny blinked, we did.

His mother stoked the hearth till it crackled merrily. Soon the smoke was rising in the hot close room, sifting through the thatch. For a second Danny worried in case the smell of roasting meat would escape too and hang over their roof like an accusation:

Here are the poachers, it would say. Here. Here. But when he heard the meat juices singing on the spit, he forgot his fears. The only thing that mattered now was to eat. To eat and eat forever. And never mind the smoke he ate with every chew, as long as those juices went on bursting and bursting in his mouth.

But all too soon when he stretched out his hand for more, Mammy stopped him.

'You'll be sick,' she said. 'After living on mangos. We must dry the rest for another day.'

In those words lurked another question: Are you really going back to the park for the rest of the meat? She gave Jacob a worried glance, but said nothing. Well what could she say? She was hungry too. What could anyone say when their fields were baked to dust and the granary empty? No one could remember a drought so bad. And yet there in the park, under their very noses was good food – herds of gazelle, impala, zebra and puku still grazing Luangwa's dying grasslands. The farmers had even owned those plains once. They were tribal lands before their one-time British rulers created the park and banned the villagers from hunting there. The ban had remained ever since, although this didn't stop the big ivory poaching gangs from invading the park. Some even said the rangers hired out their guns. And it hadn't stopped men like Dadda coming to get food for their hungry families.

More recently, though, the new government had said poaching must stop. It seemed the park was to be kept only for the foreign tourists who were suddenly flying into Mfuwe airport to stay at the new luxury safari camps. They were Americans mostly and Danny had met some when their truck bogged down in the dry stream near the house, and he and Dadda had helped dig it out. One of the white women had filmed them on a camera with a moving picture, which she told him was a camcorder. Then she'd showed him the film and Danny had seen himself as he never had before – the shy close-up smile and his chipped front tooth, then a lanky boy in the tattered grey shirt and too-short pants that he recognised as his. Behind him in the open truck sat three other tourists. They were wearing smart green safari gear and big hats and their necks were hung with binoculars and cameras with huge black lenses. Dadda wouldn't look at the film, but walked quickly away with the small kwacha note that the driver had given him for helping. Later, Danny's friend Boniface, whose father was cook at one of the safari camps, told him that the tourists had three big meals a day, and as much cake and tea as they wanted in between. All that food, they had exclaimed. It had seemed unbelievable.

When he remembered this, Danny flushed angrily. Well then, it was only fair that he and Dadda had helped themselves to an impala. Where was the harm when zebra and antelope and elephant could ignore the park boundaries and walk into their fields and eat all their crops? The villagers couldn't even kill these marauders, not even when an elephant killed a neighbour. All they could do was bang saucepans and starve.

Not now, though. Danny thought. Now they had taken matters into their own hands.

For a long time he dozed beside the hearth, reliving each mouthful of meat.

Then he fell into a dream where he and
Dadda were walking through the night.
They were back in the park. All around
them were bush sounds – a hyena
whooping, the snort of zebra, an owl. Again
Danny was afraid, but now he knew it
wasn't the wild animals that scared him –
not leopard or lion or even elephant –
because Dadda would always keep them
safe. It was something else. Some spectre
seemed to lurk at the place where they had
left their meat. Yes. Something he could not
name was waiting for them there…

Chapter Four
Ambush

Danny woke with a moan on his lips, and for the rest of the day, his dream haunted him. Yet strangely, when night fell and it was time to leave their cosy lamp-lit hut, he found his fear had gone. Now all he could think of was getting more meat. He was proud too, to be going out again with his father, the best hunter-tracker in all

Luangwa. Of course everyone in the district knew this about Jacob. For a time he had even helped the park rangers. That was in the days when the English man, Major Johnson, was still chief game warden, and he'd asked Jacob to hunt down a pride of man-eating lions that were breaking into people's huts at night and snatching hapless victims from their beds. Dadda had soon tracked the killers to their lair and dispatched all six of them, for yes he truly was the best hunter.

Danny stepped into the night with Jacob. All around the insects scraped and screeched. He followed his father's shadow over the sandy stream-bed, stepped softly across the rangers' road, then slipped through the thorn trees into the reserve. Ahead lay the sea of grass, and as Danny's eyes grew used to the dark, he choked back

a laugh. *Ha! Good old Dadda!* He'd
thought of everything. All that morning's
thatch cutting had left them a clear path
across the plain, taking them into the sage-
brush where nothing could see or smell
them for its pungent scent.

They set off quickly, bending double so
the tall grass would hide them. They were
almost running when they reached the game
trail that led to their tree. The path skirted
a river lagoon. Dead Luangwa, they called
these places, because here the river had
changed course and left behind a channel
of stagnant oily water. Fingers of white mist
coiled off it and into Danny's bones. He
shivered after the day's heat. Then suddenly
Dadda was standing stock-still, holding
Danny back. Danny peered round his
shoulder into the darkness. He sniffed the
air – a pungent, musky smell, and then

35

a rim of moon slipped from the clouds and he saw them. Elephants! A three-tonne shadow and a very small calf.

'The matriarch!' Dadda breathed. Luckily the wind was with them and Jacob pushed Danny into the sage-brush and crouched down beside him. As they watched from the bushes two more elephants pressed round the calf. They had come from the lagoon and cabbage weed and water dripped off their huge legs. Slowly, slowly, the big shapes closed round the infant. They shepherded it gently across the trail and into cover as if it were the most precious thing in the world. Danny held his breath. Mother elephants could be the meanest of all with a calf to defend. He felt Jacob's hand on his arm. The hand said, 'It's all right, boy.' And then the elephants were gone as quietly as they had come. All

Danny could hear was the retreating swish of leaves as the beasts cropped the trees.

'Come!' Jacob whispered. They hurried on along the trail, empty now except for fluttering nightjars and a porcupine hurrying home to its den. But when they drew near the mahogany tree, again Jacob grabbed Danny's arm. This time the hand said, 'Wait. Careful.' and Danny gasped. Only now did the dream's fears come flooding back. He knew why they were waiting this time – in case their decoy larder had a real leopard in it. Cold sweat trickled down his spine, and he prayed not to hear that big cat cough that froze the blood. And again he knew that he'd never make a real hunter, not like Dadda.

But then suddenly Jacob was sending him up the tree. There was no leopard, he said. Danny swung up the trunk, relief flooding his chest. As he reached the fork there was the whiff of ripe flesh. Already the ram had started to rot. He didn't care though. Here was more meat to eat and dry. It would keep them going until Father McGuire's Mission brought in the truckload of emergency supplies he had promised everyone.

Danny shoved at the hindquarters till the beast slid to the ground. He saw Dadda bend down to it and for a second hung on in the tree, flushed with triumph. He wanted to whoop and holler. *More meat. More delicious juices running down his throat.* Then the darkness flashed white and he was blinded.

'Got you!' said the voice inside the light. Danny heard the metallic click of a safety catch released. 'Dadda.'

Chapter Five
Mantrap

'Dadda!' Danny yelled again.

'Shut it!' snapped the voice. 'Come down. Slowly now.' Danny slithered to the ground at Jacob's feet, holding up his hands to fend off the light. He couldn't escape the voice though. It froze his blood as well as any leopard.

'So Jacob,' the voice sneered. 'Luangwa's best tracker has a new career?' Jacob stood his ground, 'Is a man to let his family starve so rich foreigners can come and stare at wild animals? What is one impala to them? It is elephant and lion they come to see.' Even through his fear Danny gave a silent cheer. He'd never heard his father say so much. Not all at once. And he was right. He *was*. Maybe the ranger would let them go?

But the voice only snorted and then Danny knew it: Davis Sata, the head ranger. No one in the district liked him. He had the leer of a crocodile and manners to match. There were rumours too. Ivory-poaching rumours.

The searchlight flicked off and heavy boots ground nearer. Into the dipped Land Rover headlights swaggered Davis. His brown face glistened with sweat. He was holding their rope. 'Careless,' he said, waving it under Danny's nose. 'Spotted it hanging in the thorn-bush behind the tree. And when I went to get it, what did I see? An impala in a tree. Pretending to be a leopard's kill.' Danny groaned. *This was all his stupid fault. Now they'd be going to prison for a dropped rope.*

'Been waiting these last two hours,' Davis went on.

'Better arrest me then,' Jacob said. But Davis did not answer. He stared back, the rifle resting across his forearm. 'Or I could let you go,' he said at last. He was like a cat teasing a mouse. 'In fact, you could be just the man I need, Jacob. Lost two of my best helpers last week to a charging tusker. Our elephants are growing meaner by the day. It's harder to get the ivory. But you are careful. A good tracker. You'll watch our hides and get me the merchandise. So you come, next time I call.'

Danny felt the rip of Dadda's anger. 'I'll come. But not the boy.'

'But of course the boy,' Davis laughed. 'Make a man of him. And why worry, Jacob? You've made him a poacher with this day's work.' The ranger's mouth gaped mockingly and Danny's eyes filled with tears: *All his fault. All his stupid fault.* Next Davis laid down the gun, and taking a hunting knife from his belt, hacked a leg from their ram and tossed it in the cab. 'Okay. You can go. But be ready. *Both of you.*' Then he swung into the Land Rover and roared off.

With a heart as heavy as lead-wood Danny helped Jacob sling the remains of their antelope on a branch. Between them they lugged it home and not one word did his father say, not a single word to relieve Danny's wretchedness and fear.

Nor did they have long to wait before Davis Sata came calling. In the early hours a few nights later they heard the Land Rover pull up outside their gate. Soon the latch was rattling, the arrogant thump on the door. By the light of the hurriedly-lit candle, Danny saw Jacob wave the fear from Mammy's face, tell her they'd be gone a while and not to worry. Shame pierced Danny's heart like the steel teeth of a trap. *All his fault.* Then there was no time to think. They were hustled into the back of the truck where two other man-shapes sat. The strangers did not utter a greeting or even nod. Better not to, Danny decided, although this was against all custom and only tightened his knot of fear.

The stars were fading as Davis drove them away. Danny shivered and sweated by turns. For a time they drove through dense mopane woods that closed round like a tunnel, on and on. Then they bumped across flatlands where the stumps of dead thorn trees reared up like ghosts. Danny buried his face in his arms then, while beside him Jacob sat still and comfortless as stone.

When at last the Land Rover stopped Danny found himself staring up at the biggest baobab tree he had ever seen. It reared higher than Jack's beanstalk, holding up the dark iron sky. Davis hauled Danny out. 'Up there, you!' He shoved him towards the tree. Danny stared up the trunk. Even the nearest branch was twenty feet up.

'Use the ladder, fool!' Davis pushed Danny's hands into deep scars in the tree's bark where laths had been hammered inside to make invisible rungs. 'See. Been a poacher's tree for fifty years.' He slung binoculars round Danny's neck. 'A big bull. Hundred pound tusks. Been watching him for days. Find him. Find him now.'

Danny crawled like a cockroach up the trunk, to the dizzying top where the branches spread to make a lookout post. Never had he been so far off the ground, and with the whole world laid before him. To the east, a thin red vein spread along the forest top. To the west low grey thorn-scrub stretched to Luangwa's banks. Then there was the silver snaking river and shadow trees beyond. He put the binoculars to his eyes.

'What's keeping you?' hissed Davis from below. Danny's hands shook. How could he do what the man wanted: he'd never used binoculars before? There was only a blur. Tears of fear and frustration pricked his eyes, as he turned the knob one way, then the other. Soon the sun would start to rise.

'C'mon, why don't you?'

Suddenly the dark veil fell, and Danny almost cried out. Into his sights stepped the hyena, lugging his belly home from the kill. Then behind the hyena was forest. He could even recognise some of the trees. He began to scan it, drawing the trees to him, pushing them away. That's how he found it, a lone elephant, a mile off maybe and browsing a marula tree. He stammered the details to the ranger below, saw the man strike out on foot, pushing Jacob ahead of him. Jacob's role was soon clear – to watch the wind and guide the shooter as close as possible to his quarry. Danny followed their moves from bush to bush: Jacob watching the dirt blow through his fingers, pressing quietly closer, Davis following the tracker's lead.

Danny's heart beat hard as he tried to

hold his father's image inside the binoculars. Couldn't he keep him safe in there? He knew the grim tales of what an elephant could do. He remembered their neighbour Alice. He saw Father McGuire's face flushed red with anger. He knew there were reasons enough not to poach ivory. He watched his father moving closer and closer. He saw the six-tonne bull turn towards him and lift up its trunk, sifting the air, flapping its ears. Didn't they do that before they charged?

Please Dadda. Please don't die.

Chapter Six
Ivory

Suddenly things happened very fast, like one of Father McGuire's old black and white movies that he showed every Christmas at the Mission. Danny saw Jacob snake to one side then drop into a wild-pig hole just as Davis moved forward to take his aim. There was a muffled shot, and now it was the big bull that filled the binoculars. Danny gasped.

He could see the bloody wound on its head and still it was standing! It seemed to be thinking: *Has this fire in my brain killed me?* Then it keeled over, the red dust flying.

'It's dead.' Danny said flatly to the men below. He heard the engine start up, saw the Land Rover speed out across the plain, one man hanging off the side as it veered round stumps and thorn-brush, scattering hornbills, flushing a warthog. Danny saw the men jump from the cab, axes out. Watched as they set about the bull's face, hacking the tusk roots like felling trees. When he saw the angry red holes in the elephant's cheeks, he dropped the binoculars and scrambled down the tree. He felt very cold and sick, and the question reeled in his head: weren't he and Jacob as bad as Davis? Their impala was as dead as the elephant. Yet there had to be a difference, if only he could think of the words.

When the truck drew up beside Danny, Jacob turned to shout at Davis. 'What about the meat? It will feed many hungry people.' Davis scoffed. 'Listen to Saint Jacob here. Wants to risk our necks to feed the poor!' The other men laughed, but as Danny scrambled into the truck he saw guilt flicker in their eyes. Jacob sat and glared at his feet, but Danny couldn't take his eyes off the two long rolls of gunny-sack on the truck floor. A red stain was swelling through the cloth. It was turning into a face – Davis's face, with the crocodile gape.

No one spoke again until the ranger jammed on the brakes in the middle of nowhere and told Danny and Jacob to beat it. The day was getting on, he said, and he still had the ivory to stash. 'Now remember, Jacob,' he leered, 'You come when I call.' Jacob turned on his heel and strode into the bush. Danny had to run to keep up, the wind drying his tears to salty crusts. And though it was a long way home his father did not speak once, nor even look back at him. And with every step Danny blamed himself, and re-ran the scene with the dropped rope over and over, each time carefully stuffing it in his pants, each time making a better ending. If he thought it enough times, surely it would be so.

But things only grew worse. Every day Danny saw Jacob sink into himself a little more, like a man sucked into Luangwa quicksand. Once Danny said, 'Can't we tell the Paramount Chief, Dadda?' But his father only sighed and said that when it came to ivory poaching, the stakes were high and who knew who Davis worked for or whose protection he had bought. At least he and Danny weren't in jail, or worse. But even Danny could see it was a devil's bargain, and that Jacob knew it.

Nor did the news that a truckload of emergency food supplies had arrived at the Mission lift Jacob's spirits. It was only when Danny was standing in line, waiting for Father McGuire to hand out his family's ration that he knew. This was the man to tell – the strange white man with sun-scoured cheeks and wild red hair. He was a hard man but fair and he had known Danny all his life.

And so clutching the bottle of cooking oil and bag of mealie meal, Danny waited under the mango tree in the Mission yard while the other villagers came and went. Across from him, beside the dirt road that led to the airport, was a sun-bleached billboard advertising Wonder bath soap.

Danny gazed up at the smiling woman with a handful of soapsuds, and wondered if they would be enough to wash away all his and Dadda's wrongs. Then he sniggered nervously. Not without any washing water they wouldn't.

At last he steeled himself to go back and knock on the office door, wondering what the priest would say about the poached impala and everything else. The white man had a fierce temper when roused. But then, Danny reasoned, what were a few angry words if the priest would help them. And Father McGuire would help, wouldn't he? He had to. There was no one else.

Chapter Seven
Retribution

'Son of a serpent!' cried Father McGuire
when he'd heard Danny's story. His cheeks
flushed redder than his wild red hair and he
thumped the table, while Danny shrank
into the floor. He was amazed at the old
man's fury.

After a moment the priest spoke more
calmly. 'Now Daniel, I'll not say poaching

impala is a good thing. But killing for ivory. Forcing hungry souls to commit a crime – that's breaking God's laws as well as man's.' Then he slipped into angry silence, while Danny listened to the ticking of the big wall clock and wondered if he'd done the right thing telling the priest.

At last Father McGuire smiled sadly at Danny. 'This is dangerous ground, my lad. For all of us. Just because our new president has proclaimed war on poachers, doesn't mean that there aren't more crooked officials like Sata. Someone could be protecting him. But I'll speak to the Bishop in Lusaka. He'll know who we can trust. And if he can't catch a government minister's ear, or even the President himself, and say what's going on up here, then no one can.'

The priest walked with Danny to the

Mission door, shook his hand. 'Well done, Daniel. It took courage to tell me this. Now have faith. Believe me. Davis Sata's ivory poaching days are numbered.'

At first Danny's heart soared. For a blissful moment his guilt, the dropped rope, his fear of Davis melted clean away. But then as he trailed home along the dusty road with his bag of mealie meal and bottle of oil, the doubts reared up again. What if the priest talked to the wrong people and Davis Sata got to hear? He would kill Danny for sure. Now the image of Davis with his crocodile leer seemed to fill the whole road. Now Danny knew what the frightening dream spectre was. He could name it too: Davis Sata. And now he knew that yet again he'd done the wrong thing, by telling Father McGuire.

It was two weeks before the Land Rover came for them again, just enough time to hope that Davis had let them off the hook. But no. As soon as Danny heard the night-time rap at the door, he knew they would always be at Sata's beck and call. Worse still, he had to live with the fear that the ranger would discover Danny's betrayal to Father McGuire. As he sat in the back of the truck he started to tremble. Jacob put a hand on his arm, *It's all right, boy,* but Danny couldn't tell him why he was so afraid. He saw the other two men watching them quizzically and quickly lowered his eyes.

Again they were driven to the giant baobab and again Danny was sent up the poacher's ladder. Then for an age he scanned the wooded fringes of the grassland as it emerged from darkness, wiping the cold

sweat from his brow. Below him Davis was
kicking the steel cap of his ranger's boot
against the iron trunk – thwack, thwack,
thwack. It seemed like a death sentence
and no elephant in sight. Danny prayed
for deliverance, staring out across the
empty world.

Then suddenly there it was. A big old
bull cruising the tall grass at the forest edge.
Come from nowhere. Going nowhere. Not
now. Danny focused on the wrinkled hide
that was dusted red, the battle-torn ears,
the great sweep of ivory with one tip
broken. Something about the bull's sure
steps reminded him of Dadda, and suddenly
his fear of Davis Sata flushed with fury.
Perhaps Sata wouldn't get the bull this
time. Danny prayed with all his might that
he wouldn't. Besides, it looked as if the bull
was heading towards the thorn trees near

the river. Davis would have to shoot from there if he wanted enough cover to get in close; which meant Jacob would have to swing wide, almost to the Luangwa River's banks...

He heard the ranger curse at having so much ground to cross. He was too well fed for this kind of exercise. Yet even so, he set off swiftly enough, hustling Jacob. Danny watched them creeping low through the scrub, Jacob checking the wind at every stand. While off to their right the old bull held a steady course, like a fine ship plying calm waters with no thought of the storm ahead.

Danny flicked the binoculars back and forth with growing agitation: the ranger's cruel-set jaw; Jacob's hunched shoulders. And all *he*, Danny, could do was stand in the tree and shake like a coward.

Then at last Davis was in position, taking

aim; Jacob a little way behind, crouched against a tree. It was only when the shot resounded and the elephant fell that Danny saw the second bull. It was coming the other way – *out* of the thorn trees. The first bull was still twitching and Davis fired another round, into its heart. As the gun went off the second elephant broke cover – behind Jacob.

'Da-dda!' Danny screamed. He could see the bull had his father in its sights, ears out, trunk curled across one tusk, on the charge. But the warning stuck in his throat. He could only stare in horror. Then at the last moment Jacob saw and flung himself behind the tree; and just then Davis stood up to inspect his kill. In the blink of an eye the bull had him, screaming its rage, tossing Davis like a twist of rag, piercing his cruel heart.

There was no cry from the man. And when it was done, the avenging bull stood beside his fallen comrade. He gently explored the dead grey face with the tip of his trunk, urging him to rise, while high above them, the vultures were already circling.

Danny thought his head would explode. *Dadda. Why wasn't he moving?* But suddenly there he was, snaking back through the thorn-brush, and by the time Danny had scrambled out of the tree, Dadda was slumped against the empty Land Rover, gasping for breath, his own face grey as ashes. 'Others – where?'

'Ran away. When the elephant roared.'

'Then let's go.'

Chapter Eight
All's Well...?

A few days later it was the talk of Luangwa that Davis Sata's gun, the Land Rover, and not much of Davis had been found by fellow rangers. The official story claimed he had been killed by poachers. No one believed it. No one was sorry. Secretly Danny wondered if Father McGuire had somehow caused the ranger's death. He shuddered as he recalled the ring of certainty when the priest said Davis Sata's poaching days were numbered. Or worse, perhaps his own prayers were responsible.

It wasn't long after this that the Paramount Chief of the district called a meeting at the Mission. Danny went with Jacob and a crowd of village men. They sang the national anthem and listened unmoved to the Chief's formal address until he started haranguing them about ivory poaching. Danny felt the Chief's eyes on him and shrank behind Jacob.

'It has to stop,' the Chief said. 'Our President now supports the world ban on ivory trading. But more than this, our national park is our treasure house to keep safe. Not our food store to eat bare. Tourism is a big new business for our country. You have already seen some foreign tourists, and soon there will be many more. This will create jobs for many of you. But only if there are animals in the park for the visitors to see and photograph. This means *all* poaching must stop, not just elephant hunting.'

A ripple of dissent ran round the room. The Chief held up his hand. 'I know you are hungry for meat, and especially now with no rains. Your President knows this too. He knows that even in good years we cannot keep cattle and goats up here because of tsetse fly. So in return for your promise to protect the park animals, he offers you a fair deal. He says that whenever the Wildlife Department has to cull the antelope herds, the game meat will be shared amongst you. And from now on, when foreign tourists pay to visit the park, then some of that money will be used to run your schools and clinics instead of going to central government as it used to. Yes, indeed. The President believes that we people of the Luangwa Valley should reap some real rewards from our old tribal lands, and I am sure you will be the first to agree with him.'

Danny looked around at the suddenly smiling faces. Almost everyone was murmuring their approval. Again the Chief held up his hands.

'But remember. In return, there must be no more poaching. *Of any kind.* And if you so much as smell an ivory hunter, I want to know. You take care of the animals and they'll take care of you. Right?'

'Right!' everyone chorused.

'And,' said the Chief, 'I may soon come knocking on your doors. I want to recruit a team of village game scouts to help the Wildlife Department keep poachers at bay.

I know there are some eagle-eyed trackers amongst you.'

Danny nodded, and again saw the Chief's eyes linger in their direction. This time, though, he smiled. Everyone was smiling. Even Father McGuire. Perhaps he had arranged this too. Danny turned to Jacob to see what he thought of these unexpected events. He was surprised to see the sad look in his father's eyes.

'We'd have saved ourselves much sorrow,' Jacob whispered, 'if our President had told us all these things much sooner.'

'Yes, but isn't it a good idea?' Danny urged him.

'Oh yes. It is a fine idea.'

'But Dadda, why did no one think of it before?'

Jacob shook his head. 'Who knows. Sometimes, like the baobab, wisdom is a long time growing.' Then he shrugged and added bitterly. 'Besides, we did not have these rich tourists to think of before. We only had the hunting ban. And when a man sees his family starving, he thinks only of finding meat today. He doesn't think of tomorrow.' Danny nodded grimly. He knew Dadda was right. How couldn't he know? But then didn't the Chief's words offer them some real hope, especially now they were free from Davis Sata? And he wondered why his father couldn't be more cheerful.

But later, on the way home, as they walked side by side past their neighbours' wasted gardens, Jacob turned to Danny and cried, 'I hope you've learned your lessons, boy.' Danny looked back, not understanding. Suddenly, to his amazement, Jacob's brow began to twitch with unaccustomed laughter. 'Why surely you know!' Dadda exclaimed. And when Danny still did not answer, his father said, 'Always have a tree between you and a charging elephant. And never, *ever* lose your rope.'

Now Danny laughed too. He and Jacob even danced a step on the red dust road. Above them a cloudless sky glowed blue as a china bowl, lighting up their ravaged fields. But there was still some dried impala for their supper and the Mission rations too. And soon, with luck, the rains would come and they could start to plant next year's mealies...

Author's note

The characters in the story are fictional but the setting is real. The time is 1993 during a period of a massive drought in Zambia. The place is the Luangwa Valley. This valley is the southern-most tip of the Great Rift and contains two of the world's most beautiful game parks, North and South Luangwa.

The creation of these parks meant that

rural people who once relied on game meat were effectively banished from their former traditional hunting grounds. As the valley is also infested with tsetse fly, the villagers could not replace this wild food source with domestically reared meat other than chickens. And so despite the ban, they have long resorted to game poaching to eke out a meagre diet.

In the 1970s and 80s the collapse of Zambia's primary industry, copper extraction, also fuelled large-scale commercial ivory poaching. This trade was only stemmed when the United Nations Convention for International Trade in Endangered Species banned it in 1989 causing the world value of ivory to fall, but it wasn't until 1992 that Zambia voted for a ban.

Local conservationists also campaigned to find better ways to protect the parks' wildlife, particularly elephants, before they were lost forever.

Africa's game parks cover vast territories that are difficult to police without a huge investment in arms, vehicles and personnel. Another way was needed. By involving rural farmers in eco-tourism projects, and ensuring their communities received revenue and jobs with the advent of foreign tourists, they were turned from poachers into conservationists.